For my daughter
– Ellen DeLange

For my children Luise, Oskar & Egon
– Martina Schachenhuber

Mika and the Dragonfly written by Ellen DeLange and illustrated by Martina Schachenhuber

ISBN 978-1-60537-601-1

This book was printed in March 2021 at Nikara, M. R. Štefánika 858/25, 963 01 Krupina, Slovakia.

First Edition
10 9 8 7 6 5 4 3 2 1

MIKA AND
THE DRAGONFLY

Written by
ELLEN DELANGE

Illustrated by
MARTINA SCHACHENHUBER

Clavis

NEW YORK

Mika walks along the brook and
admires the beautiful water lilies.
She looks around for stones to throw
in the water. In the distance,
she hears the loud call of bullfrogs.

Mika often comes here.
She prefers to sit under the maple tree,
with her back against the trunk.
The tree feels warm and safe.

Mika is daydreaming.
One day, she hopes to have the courage
to talk to her classmates and to play
along during recess.

She doesn't really know how to join
them. Mika is a little bit shy.

Quietly sitting in her special place, dragonflies swoop by.

Suddenly one lands on Mika's arm. Curiously, she studies the dragonfly before it flies away again. It has beautiful colored wings.

Oh no, look,
one falls on the ground!

Mika quickly walks over to the dragonfly to see what happened.

When she carefully lifts it up, she notices that one of the four wings is missing . . .

"Poor little dragonfly . . .
What can I possibly do to help you?"

She places the dragonfly on
her shoulder and walks back
home through the forest.
Tiptoeing around the prickly bushes,
she is careful not to disturb a huge
spiderweb between two trees.

Mika is mesmerized by
the dainty dragonfly.

The next day, Mika decides to bring
the dragonfly to school. During recess,
she gently carries it in her hand.
Mika is completely lost in her own
thoughts. How can she help it fly
again? She doesn't even notice
that many children have gathered
around her. Curiously, they point
at the dragonfly and ask Mika
all about it.

For a moment, Mika completely
forgets being shy. She describes
where she found the dragonfly,
explaining that it cannot fly because
it misses a wing. She tells them that
dragonflies are great aerial acrobats
and can even fly backwards . . .

Wow! The children
are very impressed by
Mika's knowledge.

When it's time to go home,
Mika skips happily down the street.

She has some great ideas
to help the dragonfly.

However, no matter what Mika tries,
the dragonfly still can't stay in the air
for long and tumbles back down
after every new attempt.

Then she remembers the spiderweb.
The intricate pattern of the spiderweb
looks so much like a dragonfly's wing.

She runs through the forest,
hoping to find the web again. There it is!
But unfortunately, it's not abandoned.
There is a big spider in it.

Sadly, this plan is not going to work either.

Mika needs some time to think
about a new idea.
When she sits in her special place,
she suddenly sees something
sparkling in the grass.

She can't believe her eyes . . .

It looks like a small wing!
Cautiously, she picks it up and runs back home.

Mika is overjoyed that she found the dragonfly's wing.
Gently she places the graceful insect on the table
and carefully glues the wing back on.
She takes the dragonfly outside to see if it can fly again . . .

The dragonfly flies up, makes a couple of small dives, then . . . it takes off! She watches it fly up high in the sky. It worked!

The next day at school, Mika is surrounded by her classmates asking her about the dragonfly. This time, Mika feels more comfortable talking with her classmates. She excitedly tells them about the dragonfly and how she was able to make it fly again.

After school, Mika runs back to the brook
to see how the dragonfly is doing.

She sits with her back against the tree,
overlooking the water, laughing at the
dragonflies making somersaults in the air.
Suddenly one lands on her nose.
Could it be her dragonfly?

From that moment on,
Mika is no longer shy.
Helping this special little friend
has given her wings of her own.